COUNT
THE
MONKEYS

ISBN 978-0-545-64148-7

Text copyright © 2013 by Mac Barnett. Illustrations copyright © 2013 by Kevin Cornell. All rights reserved. Published by Scholastic Inc., 557 Broadway, New York, NY 10012, by arrangement with Hyperion Books for Children, an imprint of Disney Book Group, LLC. SCHOLASTIC and associated logos are trademarks and/or registered trademarks of Scholastic Inc.

13 12 11 10 9 8 7 6 5 4 3   14 15 16 17 18/0

Printed in the U.S.A.   08

This edition first printing, September 2013

Book design by Whitney Manger

For Kate Sherwood
—M.B.

For Kim, who holds my hand.
—K.C.

Hey, kids! Time to count the monkeys!

It's fun. It's easy. All you have to do is turn the page . . .

and

COUNT THE MONKEYS

MAC BARNETT   KEVIN CORNELL

SCHOLASTIC INC.

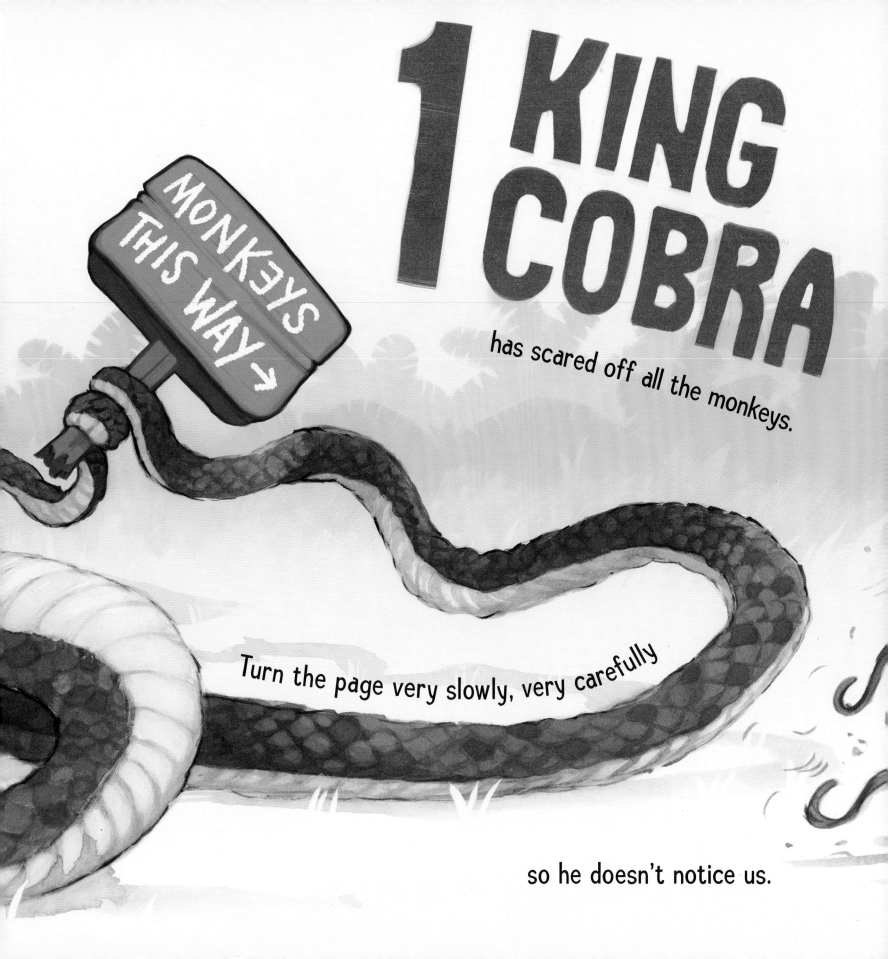

MONKEYS THIS WAY →

1 KING COBRA

has scared off all the monkeys.

Turn the page very slowly, very carefully

so he doesn't notice us.

LOOK!
2 MONGOOSES

have chased away that cobra!

Or is that **2 MONGEESE?**

I am pretty sure it is

2 MONGOOSES.

Let's vote.

Raise your hand if you think it's mongooses.
Now raise your hand if you think it's mongeese.

Interesting.

Turn the page—I bet the monkeys will come back.

Uh-oh.

3 CROCODILES

frightened those mongooses!

I dislike crocodiles, especially **these crocodiles.**

Move your hand in a *zigzag*

while you
turn the page—

it will confuse them.

We're never going to count the monkeys!

Okay. Put your arms above your head! Make a loud roar! Bang together some pots and pans, if you have them.

BUT MOST IMPORTANTLY, TURN THAT PAGE!

OH NO!
5 BEE SWARMS
drove off those bears.

Bees can smell fear.

You are not afraid, are you?

Hum a happy tune and smile
while you turn that page.

Phew! **6 SWEET OLD BEEKEEPERS** have shooed off all those bees.

Say "thank you" six times, very politely—
these ladies care about good manners.

Now,
finally,
the monkeys
can
come
back.

Turn the page and count the monkeys!

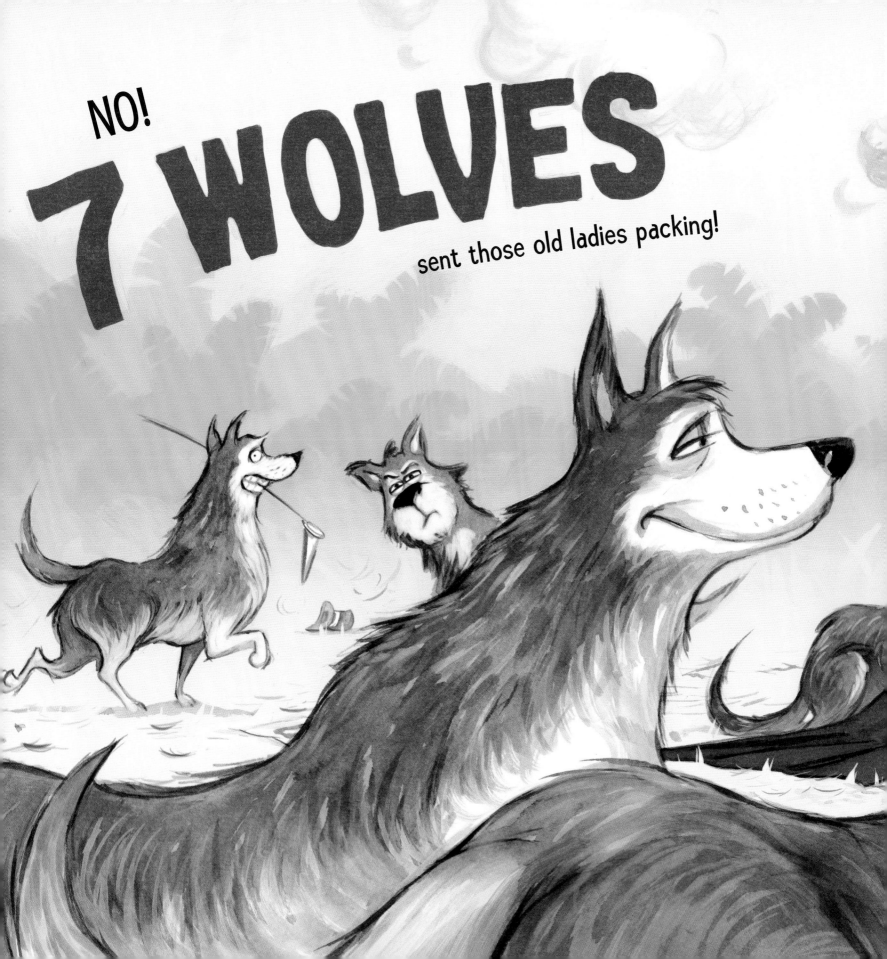

Wolves and grandmas never get along!

This is very important: **Don't look** these wolves in the eyes.

In fact, cover your eyes while you turn the page.

Oh good.

8 LUMBERJACKS

took care of those wolves.

Thanks, guys!
Now it's safe for the monkeys.

Give each lumberjack
a high five
and then turn the page

so we can

COUNT
THE
MONKEYS.

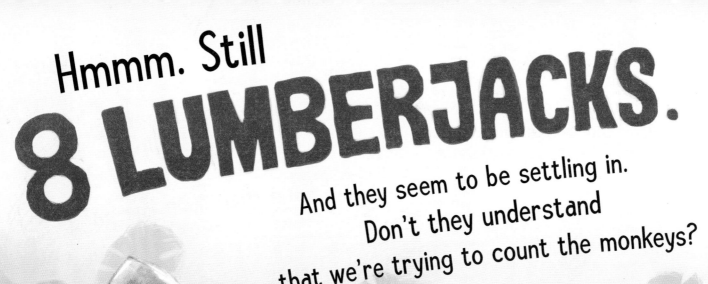

Hmmm. Still 8 LUMBERJACKS.

And they seem to be settling in.
Don't they understand
that we're trying to count the monkeys?

Great.
9 LUMBERJACKS.

They invited a friend.

Look at that!

10 POLKA-DOTTED RHINOCEROSES WITH BAGPIPES AND BAD BREATH cleared out those lumberjacks.

Was that your idea?

Because it wasn't mine.

Okay! We're finally ready to—
Oh no. It looks like we're
out of pages.

This is terrible!
We made it to the end
and there are

O MONKEYS

in this book.

Now we'll never get to count the monkeys.

MAC BARNETT is ONE man who has written THIRTEEN books, including *Billy Twitters and His Blue Whale Problem*, *Mustache!*, *Chloe and the Lion*, and *Extra Yarn*, winner of the *Boston Globe–Horn Book Award*. He also writes the Brixton Brothers mystery series. Mac lives in the EIGHTH-largest city of the THIRTY-FIRST state, which is Oakland, California. Visit him a MILLION times at www.macbarnett.com.

Despite having dedicated half his life to drawing monkeys, this is the first time Philadelphia illustrator **KEVIN CORNELL** has drawn ones not made of socks. To see other non-sock animals Kevin has drawn, check out *The Trouble with Chickens* by Doreen Cronin, and *Mustache!* by Mac Barnett. Visit www.kevskinrug.com to explain to him that mustaches are not animals.